LET'S PLAY CARDS!

To R. A. K. and J. M. S.—true card sharks.

—E. S.

This book is for Deanna & Philip, Katherine & Gail, Leepie & Peetie, Stevie & Blackie, Mayzie & Mia! Lots of huge THANK YOUs to Mikey, Julie, Lindley, Lee, Ann, Chani & Ruth!

—J. K.

First Aladdin Paperbacks Edition, 1996
Text copyright © 1996 by Elizabeth Silbaugh
Illustrations copyright © 1996 by Jef Kaminsky

Aladdin Paperbacks
An imprint of Simon & Schuster Children's Publishing Division
1230 Avenue of the Americas
New York, NY 10020

Manufactured in the United States of America
10 9 8 7 6 5 4 3 2 1

The Library of Congress has cataloged the Simon & Schuster Books for Young Readers
Edition as follows:
Silbaugh, Elizabeth.
Let's Play Cards! : a first book of card games / by Elizabeth Silbaugh ;
illustrated by Jef Kaminsky.
p.   cm. — (Ready-to-Read)
Summary: Provides a simple introduction to playing cards and directions for the
games of War, Concentration, Go Fish, Crazy Eights, and Clock Solitaire.
1. Card games—Juvenile literature. [1. Card games. 2. Games.]
I. Kaminsky, Jef, ill. II. Title. III. Series.
GV1244.S55   1996
795.4—dc20   96-596
CIP   AC
ISBN 0-689-80802-X (hc)   ISBN 0-689-80801-1 (pbk)

LET'S PLAY CARDS!

A FIRST BOOK OF CARD GAMES

By Elizabeth Silbaugh
Illustrated by Jef Kaminsky

Ready-to-Read
Aladdin Paperbacks

Outside, it's a cold, rainy night.
Inside, it's cozy and warm.
You are sipping cocoa.

What will you do for fun?
Suddenly, you have an idea.
"Let's play cards!"

Some card games are silly.

Some card games are serious.

You can play cards by yourself.

You can play cards with another person.
Or you can play cards in a group.
This book will get you started.
All you need is a little patience—
and a deck of cards!

Cool Carl the
Card Shark, here!
I'll add some POINTERS
from time to time!

Before you start playing,
you should know a few things.
A complete deck has 52 cards.
Thirteen of them are spades.
Thirteen of them are hearts.

Thirteen of them are diamonds.
Thirteen of them are clubs.
Spades, hearts, diamonds, and clubs
are called "suits."

Some decks have
an extra two cards.
These are the Jokers.
Jokers don't have suits.

Now take a look at the numbers
and letters on the cards.
In each suit, you will see
cards numbered from two to ten.
You will also see
four special cards in each suit.
Three of these are called "face cards."
The King is the highest.
The Queen comes next, then the Jack.
All the face cards are higher than
the cards with numbers.
The last special card is the Ace.
It has the letter A in the corners.

See the faces?
Not quite enough
teeth for my taste, but . . .
In some games, the Ace
is the highest card of all.
But in other games, the
Ace acts like a one.

11

To play most card games, you
need to practice three things.

1. Shuffling the cards.
Here are some good ways.

Pile-shuffle. Just dump the
cards on the table and mix
them around.

Cut-shuffle. Hold the pack in
one hand. With the other
hand, lift off a few cards
and gently push them back
into the rest of the pack.

Flutter-shuffle. Grasp half
of the pack flat in each
hand. Use your thumbs
to flutter the two halves
into each other.

2. Dealing the cards.
If you are the dealer, give a card face-down
to each player, starting on your left.
Give one to yourself last.
Always deal from
the top of the deck.

3. Holding the
cards in a fan.
The cards you are dealt
are called your "hand."
To keep other players from seeing what
you have, make a fan.
First, hold your cards in a pack;
then slide them around into a half circle.
Be sure to hold the fan up so
no one can peek!

Are you ready to start playing? Good!

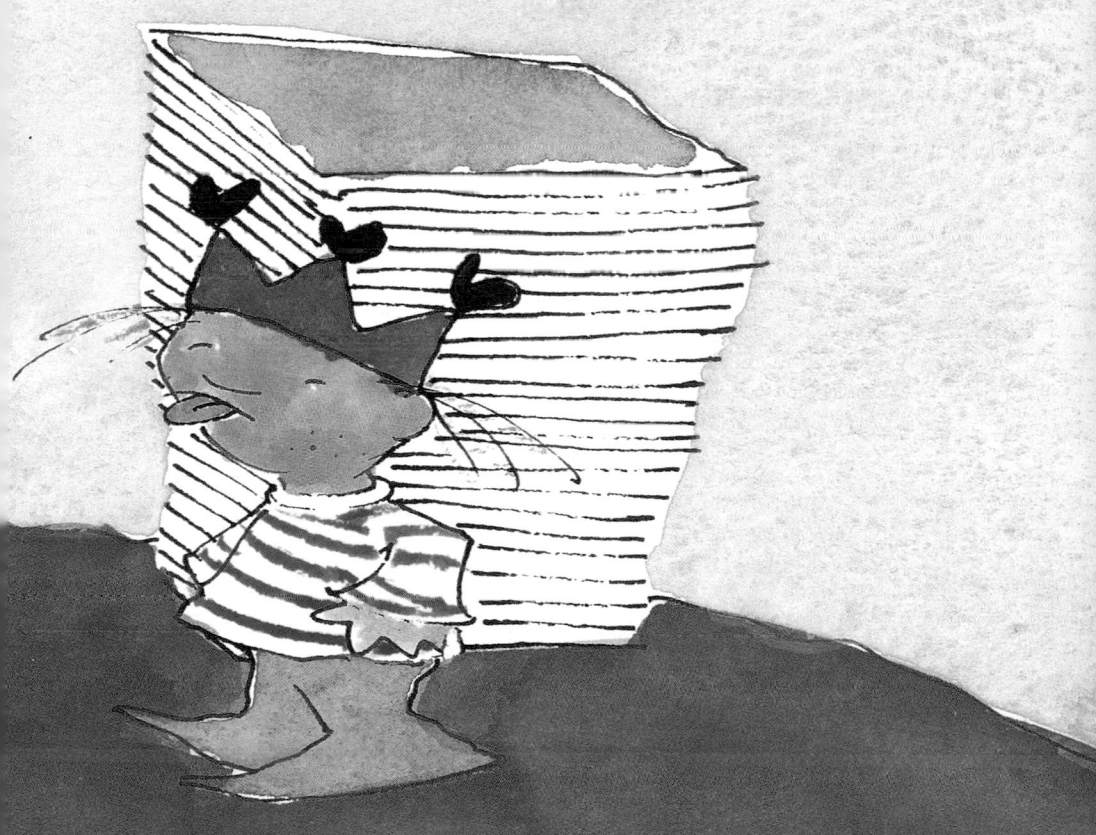

You won't use a fan here.

Game #1: WAR

Number of players: 2

Shuffle the cards and
deal out the whole deck.

Now you each have 26 cards.

Don't look at your cards.

Just hold them in a pack, face-down.

Touch the top card on your pack.
At the count of three,
flip the top card face-up onto the table.
Both players do this at the same time.

Is your card higher?
Yes! You win both cards!
Slide them onto the bottom
of your pack.
Keep flipping cards face-up
and seeing who wins.

By the way, in this game,
Jokers are the highest.
Aces are the next highest,
then the face cards.

Now for the tricky part.

What if the flipped cards are the same?

Let's say you both turned up Jacks.

It's time for a *War!*

Each of you deals three cards

face-down from the top of your pack.

At the count of three,
flip the fourth card face-up.
Whose is higher?
The winner takes all ten cards.

Snatched from
the jaws of defeat!

If those fourth cards are the same,
it's time for a *Double War!*
Both of you lay down three more cards.
Flip the fourth one face-up.
The winner takes all 18 cards!
To win a game of War,
you must get every card in the deck.

War can take a long time.
Pour some cocoa,
and have fun!

Do you know what "good
sportsmanship" is?
It is remembering
not to gloat too much.
We all win some;
we all lose some.

21

CONCENTRATION

GAME #2: CONCENTRATION

Number of players: 2 or more

Do you have a good memory?

If so, you'll be great at Concentration!

If not, your memory will improve

the more you play the game.

For this game, you need

a good smooth surface,

free of toys, dogs, and other obstacles.

Start by shuffling the cards, as usual.
Then lay out the whole deck
face-down in rows.
When it is your turn,
flip over any two cards.
Do they make a pair?
A pair is two cards with
matching letters or numbers.
If you did not get a pair,
flip the cards back over.
That's the end of your turn.
If you *did* turn up a pair,
take the cards out of the rows.
Stash them away by your side.
You get to go again—right now.

No, no, no, you shrimp!
Not that kind of pear!

There are d'Anjou,
Bartlett, and many
other kinds of delicious
pears out there.

During other
players' turns,
try to concentrate
on which cards they flip over.
Your good memory will help you
on your next turn!

When all the cards have been taken,
count up your pairs.
You guessed it:
the player with the most cards wins.

Want to play again?
To make it harder, don't
lay the cards in an even grid.
Put them every which way.
Be sure to shuffle well,
and keep that playing surface clear.

You're doing swimmingly!

GAME #3: GO FISH

Number of players: 3, 4, or 5

Like Concentration, the object of Go Fish
is to get as many pairs as possible.
But this time you will be "fishing"
from other players' hands
for matching cards.

Deal five cards to each player.
The stack of leftover cards goes
in the middle of the table, face-down.
Hold your cards in a fan.
Do you see any pairs?

If you do, put them down
on the table in front of you.
If you do not, you will have to
wait your turn to "go fish."

Give that
kid a "hand"!

As the dealer, you go first.
Ask another player for a card
that matches one you already have.
For example, let's say
you have a Queen in your hand.
You would pick another player and ask,
"Molly, do you have a Queen?"

If Molly has the card,
she must hand it over.
Put your new pair down
in front of you.
Now you get to go again!
Pick any player and ask for
another card.
If the player you picked does
not have it,
he says, *"Go fish!"*
Then you must draw a card
from the stack.
This is the end of your turn.

If you happen to pick
the exact card you
were asking for,
take another turn!

Listen carefully when other
players ask for cards.
Remember, they can
only ask for cards
they already have.
Try to figure out who is
holding the cards you need.

Then you will know where
to go fishing!
The game ends when any
player runs out of cards.
Count your pairs.
Whoever has the most wins!

Remember, hold your
cards up so no
one else can
see them!

GAME #4: CRAZY EIGHTS

Number of players: 2, 3, or 4

When is an eight not an eight?

In Crazy Eights!

Everyone can be a magician

Don't worry. You'll see what that means in a minute.

in this wacky game.

First, deal eight cards to each player.

Place the rest of the cards in a stack

in the middle of the table.

Take the top card off

Flip!

the stack and lay

it face up

beside the stack.

In this game, players hold

their cards in fans.

If you are the dealer,
you get to go first.

I go first!
Me, me, me!!!

Look at the card in the middle
of the table.
You must play one of your cards
on top of it.
But you can't play just any old card.
Your card must match that card.
It must either be the same number
or the same suit.

Uh-oh! You have no cards that work.
You will have to draw cards
from the stack
until you get one that you can play.

Sometimes you'll be holding
a lot of cards in your hand.
Don't worry. Slowly but surely,
you'll get rid of them!

But wait!

Do you have an eight? *Any* eight?

This is what Crazy Eights is all about!

If you have an eight in your hand, or

if you draw one from the deck,

you can play it.

You can also make it any suit.
If you have a lot of clubs to play,
say, "This eight is clubs," even if the
eight is a diamond.

Thank goodness for magic eights!

Presto!

What if the middle stack
runs out of cards?
Then the dealer picks up the stack
of face-up cards. He leaves the
top card face-up on the table and
shuffles the rest of the pack.

These form the new pile to draw from.
Who wins? The first player to run
out of cards!

Watch out! It's hard to STOP
playing Crazy Eights
once you start!

CLOCK SOLITAIRE

GAME #5:
CLOCK SOLITAIRE
Number of players: 1
Are you all by yourself?
Do you still want to play
cards?

Some games work for one player.
These are called Solitaire.
Start with a simple Solitaire game
called Clock.

After shuffling the cards,
deal them into 13 face-down piles.
Twelve piles should form a circle
like the numbers on a clock.
Put the last pile in the middle.
There will be four cards in each pile.
Now turn up the top card
of the middle pile.
Where does it belong?
If it is a seven,
it goes at seven o'clock.

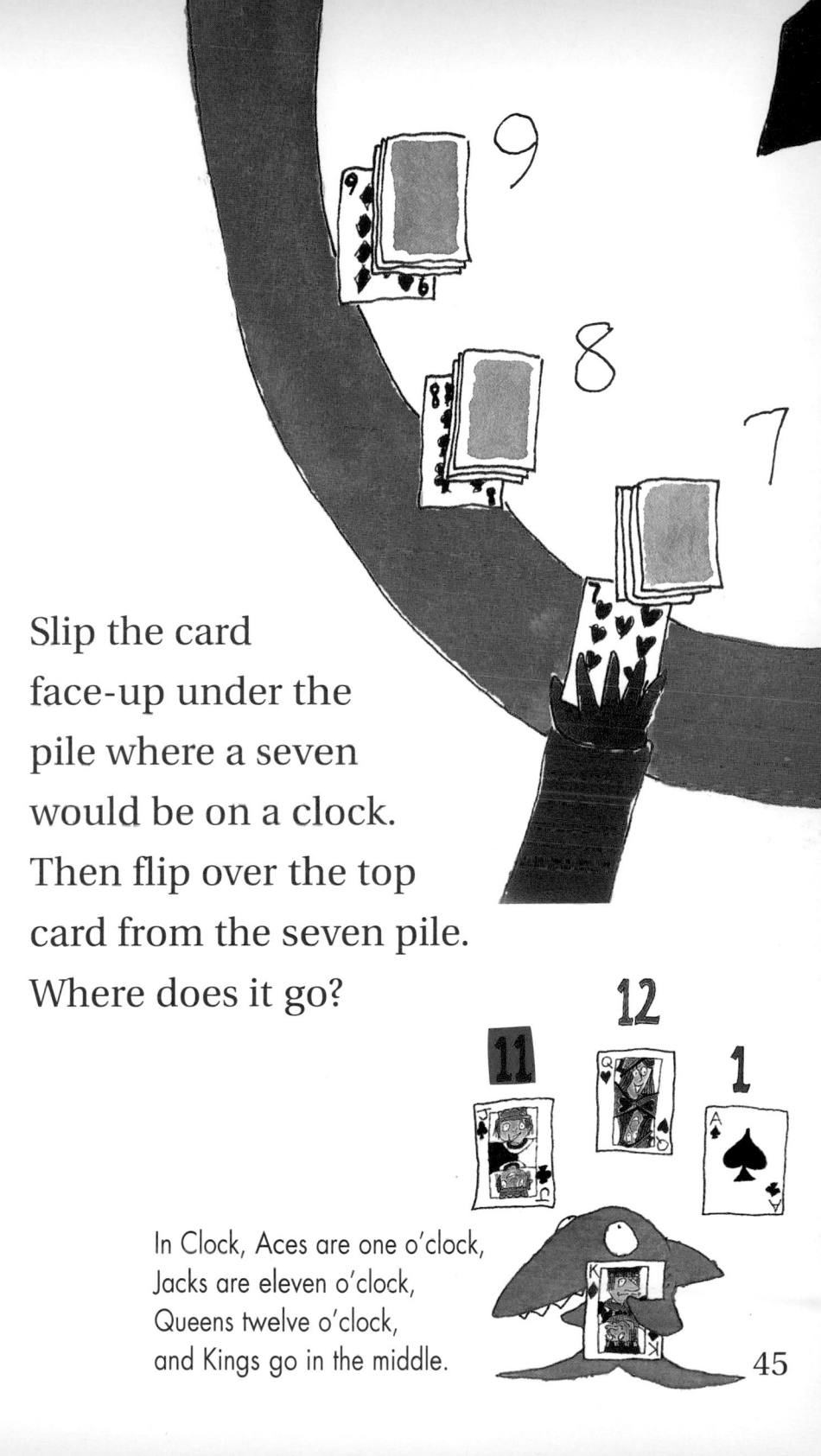

Slip the card
face-up under the
pile where a seven
would be on a clock.
Then flip over the top
card from the seven pile.
Where does it go?

In Clock, Aces are one o'clock,
Jacks are eleven o'clock,
Queens twelve o'clock,
and Kings go in the middle.

45

Keep sliding cards under and
taking cards off the tops of piles.
When you get to the last
face-down cards,
the numbers on the clock
face will appear.
But watch out for the Kings!
If all four of them reach
the center before the other
piles are done, the game ends.
It's time to deal out another clock!

You're sunk!
You're FIN-ished!

Now you know how to play
a few card games.
Ask your family and friends
to teach you more.
Then you will become
a card shark, too!

Bye!

MORE OF JANICE VANCLEAVE'S
WILD, WACKY, AND WEIRD
PHYSICS
EXPERIMENTS

Illustrations by
Lorna William

ROSEN
PUBLISHING

NEW YORK

This edition published in 2017 by
The Rosen Publishing Group, Inc.
29 East 21st Street
New York, NY 10010

Library of Congress Cataloging-in-Publication Data

Names: VanCleave, Janice.
Title: More of Janice VanCleave's wild, wacky, and weird physics experiments / Janice VanCleave.
Description: New York : Rosen YA, 2017. | Series: Janice Vancleave's wild, wacky, and weird science experiments | Includes index.
Identifiers: LCCN ISBN 9781499465532 (pbk.) | ISBN 9781499465556 (library bound) | ISBN 9781499465549 (6-pack)
Subjects: LCSH: Physics—Experiments—Juvenile literature.
Classification: LCC QC25.V364 2016 | DDC 530.078—dc23

Manufactured in the United States of America

Illustrations by Lorna William

Experiments first published in *Janice VanCleave's 202 Oozing, Bubbling, Dripping, and Bouncing Experiments* by John Wiley & Sons, Inc. copyright © 1996 Janice VanCleave and *Janice VanCleave's 200 Gooey, Slippery, Slimy, Weird and Fun Experiments* by John Wiley & Sons, Inc. copyright © 1992 Janice VanCleave

CONTENTS

INTRODUCTION

Physics is the study of energy, matter, and forces and their relationship with each other. Physicists study everything from tiny atomic particles to the whole universe! Albert Einstein (1879–1955) is perhaps the most famous physicist, and many choose to follow in his footsteps.

The people who decide to work in the field of physics have a variety of career choices. Some engineers investigate aircraft accidents and others work with nuclear power. Some physicists design high-speed trains, roller coasters, or lasers for surgery. All of these people have something in common: they are constantly asking questions to learn even more about physics.

This book is a collection of science experiments about physics. How does sound travel? How does an inclined plane make work easier? Does shape affect an object's strength? You will find the answers to these and many other questions by doing the experiments in this book.

HOW TO USE THIS BOOK

You will be rewarded with successful experiments if you read each experiment carefully, follow the steps in order, and do not substitute materials. The following sections are included for all the experiments.

» **PURPOSE:** *The basic goals for the experiment.*

» **MATERIALS:** *A list of supplies you will need.* You will experience less frustration and more fun if you gather all the necessary materials for the experiments before you begin. You lose your train of thought when you have to stop and search for supplies.

» **PROCEDURE:** *Step-by-step instructions on how to perform the experiment.* Follow each step very carefully, never skip steps, and do not add your own. Safety is of the utmost importance, and by reading the experiment before starting, then following the instructions exactly, you can feel confident that no unexpected results will occur. Ask an adult to help you when you are working with anything sharp or hot. If adult supervision is required, it will be noted in the experiment.

» **RESULTS:** *An explanation stating exactly what is expected to happen.* This is an immediate learning tool. If the expected results are achieved, you will know that you did the experiment correctly. If your results are not the same as described in the experiment, carefully read the instructions and start over from the first step.

WHY? *An explanation of why the results were achieved.*

INTRODUCTION

THE SCIENTIFIC METHOD

Scientists identify a problem or observe an event. Then they seek solutions or explanations through research and experimentation. By doing the experiments in this book, you will learn to follow experimental steps and make observations. You will also learn many scientific principles that have to do with physics.

In the process, the things you see or learn may lead you to new questions. For example, perhaps you have completed the experiment that studies how string length affects the sound of stringed instruments. Now you wonder what affect string thickness has. That's great! All scientists are curious and ask new questions about what they learn. When you design a new experiment, it is a good idea to follow the scientific method.

1. Ask a question.

2. Do some research about your question. What do you already know?

3. Come up with a hypothesis, or a possible answer to your question.

4. Design an experiment to test your hypothesis. Make sure the experiment is repeatable.

5. Collect the data and make observations.

6. Analyze your results.

7. Reach a conclusion. Did your results support your hypothesis?

Many times the experiment leads to more questions and a new experiment.

Always remember that when devising your own science experiment, have a knowledgeable adult review it with you before trying it out. Ask them to supervise it as well.

BEST SPOT

PURPOSE To determine whether the position of a lever's fulcrum affects the lever.

MATERIALS ruler
　　　　　　pencil
　　　　　　30 pennies

PROCEDURE

1. Make a lever by laying the 4-inch (10-cm) mark of the ruler across the pencil.

2. Place 10 pennies between the zero end of the ruler and the 1-inch (2.5-cm) mark. This will be called end B.

3. Add and record the number of pennies needed on the opposite end of the ruler end A to lift the 10 pennies.

4. Move the pencil to the 8-inch (20-cm) mark.

5. Add and record the number of pennies needed on end A to lift the 10 pennies.

RESULTS It took many more pennies to lift the 10 pennies when the pencil was at the 8-inch (20-cm) mark.

WHY? The ruler and pencil form a lever. The pencil acts as the fulcrum. In this experiment, the effort force was the stack of pennies needed to lift the 10 pennies. The longer the distance from the point of effort to the fulcrum, the less effort force needed to move the object on the other end.

8

9

Best Spot

PUMPS

PURPOSE To demonstrate how a wheel can be used as a pump.

MATERIALS drawing compass
ruler
poster board
scissors
round toothpick
eyedropper
tap water
adult helper

PROCEDURE

1. Use the compass to draw a circle with a 4-inch (10-cm) diameter on the poster board.

2. Cut out the circle.

3. Ask an adult to insert about one-third of the toothpick through the center of the circle to form a top.

4. Fill the eyedropper with water.

5. Ask your helper to spin the top.

6. Hold the eyedropper above the top and drop water onto the spinning circle.

7. Observe the movement of the water.

RESULTS The water sprays out in all directions.

WHY? The falling water is thrown away from the spinning circle. If you could slow down the motion of the water, you would see that the water leaves the spinning top in a straight line. Spinning materials, if free to move, are thrown off in a straight line. This knowledge was used to design a simple machine to pump water. Water flowing onto a spinning metal disk creates a wheel pump that very effectively pumps water from one spot to another.

Inclined

PURPOSE To determine if an inclined plane makes work easier.

MATERIALS 12-inch (30-cm) piece of string
rubber band
8-ounce (236-ml) glue bottle
2 books
ruler

PROCEDURE

1. Loop the string through the rubber band and attach the string to the top of the glue bottle.

2. Lay the books on a table.

3. Raise the end of one book and rest it on top of the second book.

4. Place the glue bottle on the table near the flat book.

5. Hold the rubber band and lift the bottle of glue straight up and place it on the book.

6. Use the ruler to measure how much the rubber band stretches.

7. Lay the glue bottle at the bottom of the inclined book.

8. Hold the rubber band and pull the bottle until it reaches the height of the flat book.

9. Measure with the ruler how much the rubber band stretches.

RESULTS The rubber band stretches the most when the bottle is lifted straight up.

WHY? You lifted the glue bottle to the same height each time, but lifting it straight up took more effort because you were holding the entire weight of the bottle. The books form a simple machine called an inclined plane that helps to support some of the weight of the bottle. You had to pull the bottle up the incline a longer distance to reach the height of the book, but it took much less effort, as shown by the rubber band that stretched less.

WATER PRISM

PURPOSE To use water to disperse light into its separate colors.

MATERIALS

scissors

heavy paper

ruler

masking tape

clear drinking glass

tap water

chair

sheet of printer paper

flashlight

helper

PROCEDURE

1. Cut a circle from the heavy paper to cover the end of the flashlight.

2. Cut a very thin slit across the circle, stopping about 1/2 inch (1.25 cm) from each edge.

3. Tape the paper circle to the front of the flashlight.

4. Fill the glass about three-fourths full with water.

5. Place the glass of water on the edge of the chair.

6. Have your helper hold the heavy paper near the floor at the edge of the chair.

7. Darken the room and hold the flashlight at an angle to the surface of the water.

8. Change the angle of the flashlight and ask your helper to vary the position of the paper.

9. Look for colors on the paper.

RESULTS A spectrum of colors is seen on the paper.

WHY? White light contains all of the visible spectrum colors—red, orange, yellow, green, blue, indigo, and violet. Light can be dispersed (separated into the spectrum colors) by passing it through different substances such as water or glass. Dispersion occurs because the different colors of light in white light are refracted, or bent, by the substance through which they pass.

15

Water Prism

STARBURST

PURPOSE To demonstrate how a diffraction grating affects light.

MATERIALS lamp
cotton handkerchief

PROCEDURE

1. Remove the shade from the lamp.

2. Stand about 6 feet (2 m) from the glowing bulb.

3. Hold the handkerchief at eye level and stretch it with both hands.

4. Look at the light through the stretched cloth.

RESULTS A starburst of light with dim bands of yellow and orange colors appears around the light.

WHY? The cloth acts like a diffraction grating, which disperses light—separates light into the colors of the visible spectrum. Diffraction gratings are made by using a diamond point to cut as many as 12,000 lines per 1/2 inch (1.25 cm) on a piece of glass or plastic. The spaces between the woven threads in the cloth separate the light, but since the holes in the weave are large, not as many separate colors are seen as one would observe through a diamond-cut grating.

BLINKER

PURPOSE To demonstrate the strobe effect of a television picture.

MATERIALS television
pencil

PROCEDURE

1. With the lights on, swing the pencil up and down quickly and observe how it looks.

2. With only the television on, hold the pencil in front of the screen.

3. Quickly swing the pencil up and down 4 to 5 times.

RESULTS In light, the moving pencil produces a continuous blur. In front of the television screen, separate images of the pencil are seen in different places.

WHY? Separate images of the pencil are seen in front of the television because the light from the television screen is not constant. Many pictures are flashed on the screen each second. Between the pictures the screen goes black, and the movement of the pencil is not seen. This blinking light gives the illusion that the pencil is moving in slow motion. You do not notice any blinking while watching television because your eyes retain the image of each picture long enough to receive the flashing of the next picture.

Blinker

SOUND BLASTER

PURPOSE To demonstrate stereophonic sound.

MATERIALS 36-inch (1-m) piece of string
wire coat hanger
metal spoon
helper

PROCEDURE

1. Wrap the ends of the string around your index fingers.

2. Place your fingers in your ears.

3. Hang the hook of the hanger in the middle.

4. Lean over so that the hanger hangs freely.

5. Ask your helper to use the spoon to tap the hanger several times.

RESULTS A loud chiming sound is heard.

WHY? All sound is a form of wave motion that is produced when objects vibrate. Striking the hanger causes it to vibrate. The vibrations travel through the air and up the string to your ears. This is an example of stereophonic sound, which is when different sounds come toward a listener from two different directions. The sounds traveling up the string are slightly different and each sound is directed toward a different ear.

Sound Blaster

CUP TELEPHONE

PURPOSE To demonstrate how sound travels.

MATERIALS pencil
two 7-ounce (210-ml) paper cups
9-yard (8-m) piece of string
helper

PROCEDURE

1. Use the pencil to make a small hole in the bottom of each cup.

2. Thread the ends of the string through the holes in the cups.

3. Knot each end of the string to keep them from pulling through the holes.

4. Have your helper hold one cup while you hold the other. Hold the cups by placing your thumb and index finger on the rim.

5. Walk away from your helper until the string is stretched tightly between you.

6. Hold the cup to your ear while your helper speaks softly into the other cup.

RESULTS Your helper's words are loud and clear.

WHY? Sound can travel through solid objects like paper cups and string. Sounds are made by vibrating objects. The vibrating vocal cords in your helper's throat cause air molecules to vibrate. These vibrating air molecules make the cup vibrate. The vibrating cup makes the string vibrate, and the string passes the vibrations on to your cup. You hear the vibrations as your helper's words.

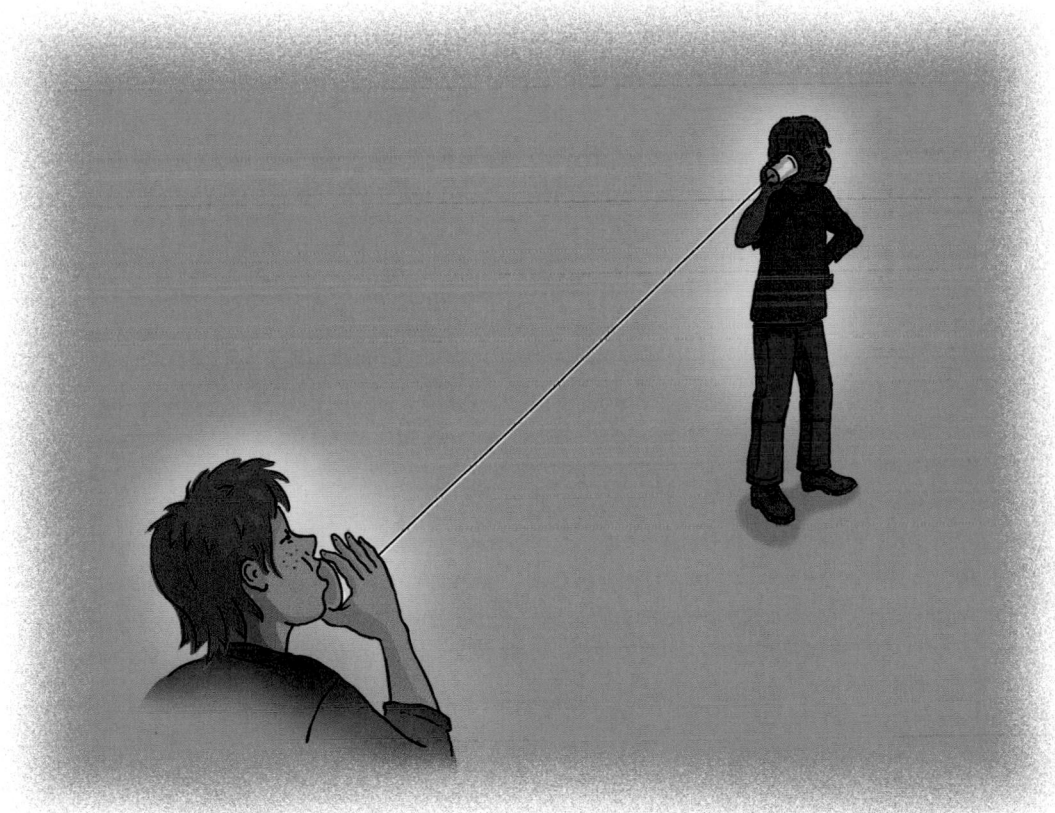

STRING MUSIC

PURPOSE To determine how tension in a string affects the sound of stringed instruments.

MATERIALS 6-foot (2-m) piece of strong string
2 buckets with handles (1-quart [1-liter] is large enough)
2 pencils
enough rocks to fill both buckets

PROCEDURE

1. Follow these steps to prepare a model of a stringed instrument:

   » Place the string across a table that is about 3 feet (1 m) wide, and tie the ends to the bucket handles so that the buckets hang freely.

   » Place the pencils under the string on both edges of the table.

   » Fill each bucket halfway with rocks.

2. Observe the sound produced as you pluck the center of the string with your fingers.

3. Fill the buckets with the remaining rocks.

4. Again, observe the sound produced as you pluck the center of the string.

NOTE: Keep the model stringed instrument for the next experiment.

RESULTS Adding more rocks to the bucket produced a higher sound.

WHY? Adding weight to the buckets increases the tightness or tension (condition of being stretched) in the string. As the tension of the string increases, the string vibrates faster when plucked, which produces a higher-pitched sound.

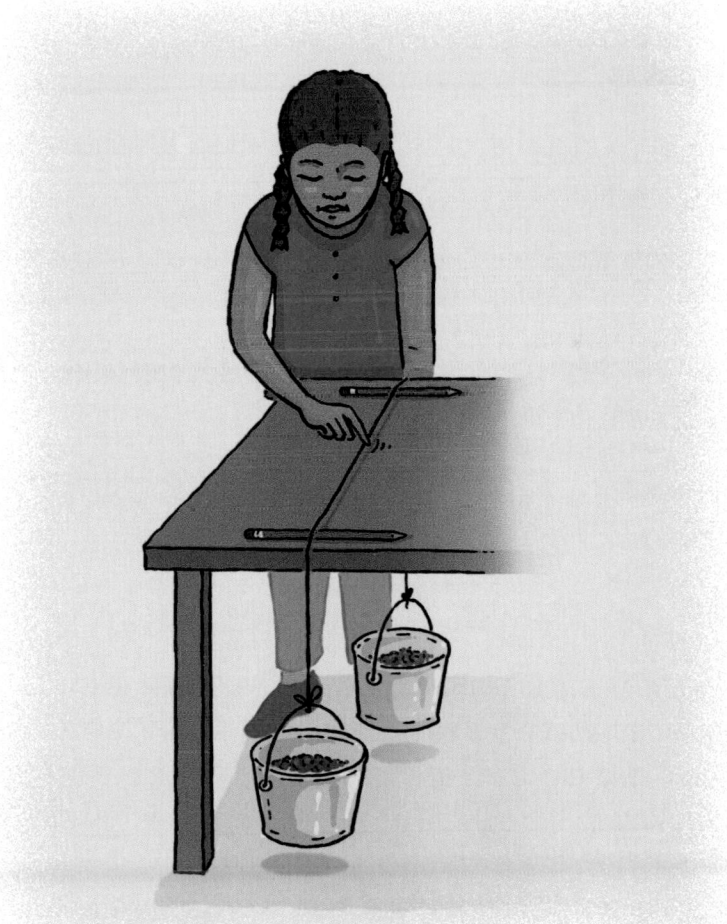

STREAMERS

PURPOSE To charge an object with static electricity.

MATERIALS scissors
ruler
tissue paper
comb

PROCEDURE

1. Measure and cut a strip of tissue paper about 3 inches x 10 inches (7.5 cm x 25 cm).

2. Cut long, thin strips in the paper, leaving one end uncut (see diagram).

3. Quickly move the comb through your hair several times. Your hair must be clean, dry, and oil-free.

4. Hold the teeth of the comb near, but not touching, the cut end of the paper strips.

RESULTS The thin paper strips move toward the comb.

WHY? "Static" means "stationary." Static electricity is the buildup of negative charges, which are called electrons. Matter is made up of atoms, which have electrons spinning around a positive center called the nucleus. Moving the comb through your hair actually rubs electrons off the hair and onto the comb. The side of the comb that touched your hair has a build-up of electrons, making that side negatively charged. The paper strip is made of atoms. Holding the negatively charged comb close to the paper causes the positive part of the atoms in the paper to be attracted to the comb. This attraction between negative and positive charges is strong enough to lift individual strands of paper.

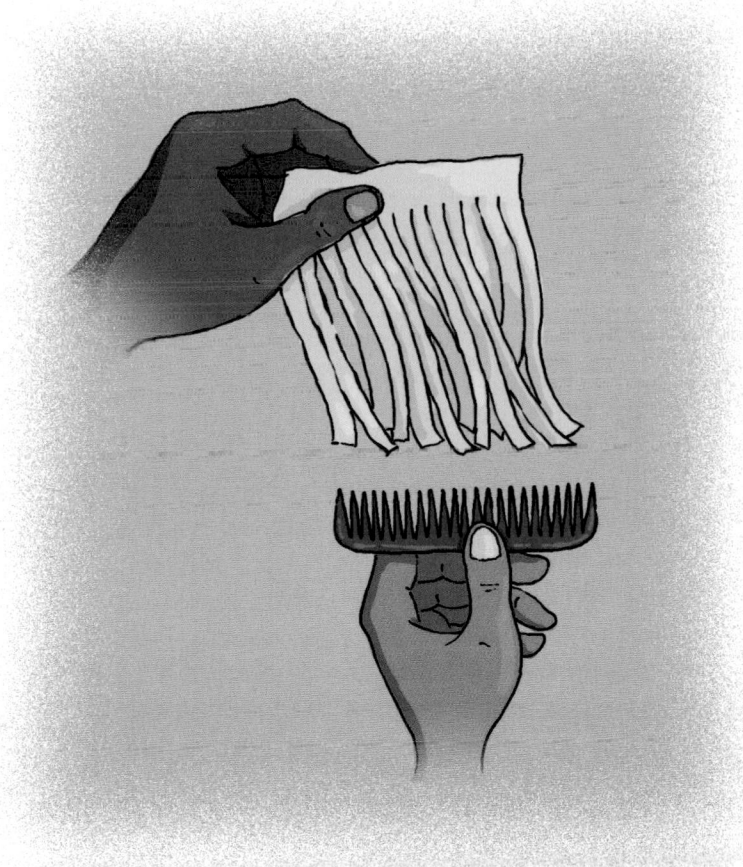

SNAP

PURPOSE To demonstrate how static charges produce sound.

MATERIALS clear plastic sheet
scissors
ruler
modeling clay
large paper clip
piece of wool: a scarf, coat, or sweater made of 100%
wool will work

PROCEDURE

1. Measure and cut a plastic strip about 1 inch x 8 inches (2.5 cm x 20 cm).

2. Use the clay to stand the paper clip upright on a table.

3. Wrap the wool around the plastic strip and quickly pull the plastic through the cloth. Do this quickly at least three times.

4. Immediately hold the plastic near the top of the paper clip.

RESULTS A snapping sound can be heard.

WHY? Electrons are rubbed off the wool and onto the plastic. The electrons clump together until the addition of their energy is great enough to move them across the span of air between the plastic and the metal clip. The movement of the electrons through the air produces sound waves, resulting in the snapping sound heard.

SUSPENDED AIRPLANE

PURPOSE To use magnetic force to suspend a paper airplane.

MATERIALS tissue paper
steel straight pin
scissors
bar magnet
ruler
sewing thread, 12 inches (30 cm)

PROCEDURE

1. Measure and cut a small wing about 1 inch (2.5 cm) long from the paper.

2. Insert the pin through the center of the paper wing to make an "airplane."

3. Tie the thread to the head of the pin.

4. Place the magnet on the edge of a table with the end of the magnet extending over the edge of the table.

5. Place the airplane on the end of the magnet.

6. Slowly pull on the string until the airplane is suspended in the air.

RESULTS The airplane remains airborne as long as it stays close to the magnet.

WHY? The strength of attraction between two magnets depends on how orderly the magnetic domains (clusters of atoms that behave like tiny atoms) are in the magnets. The atoms in the pin are randomly arranged before the pin touches the magnet. The number of atoms that arrange themselves into clusters (domains) and line up in the pin when it is placed on the magnet depends on the strength of the magnet. The pin and magnet both have magnetic properties. They pull on each other with enough force to overcome the downward pull of gravity, which allows the airplane to remain suspended.

FORCE FIELD

PURPOSE To demonstrate the pattern of magnetic force fields around magnets of different shapes.

MATERIALS magnets, a variety—round, bar, U-shaped

iron filings: ask an adult to buy them online or at an office supply store.

paper cup

notebook paper

PROCEDURE

1. Pour the iron filings into the paper cup.

2. Place the magnets on a table.

3. Cover the magnets with a sheet of paper.

4. Sprinkle a thin layer of iron filings on the paper over the magnets.

5. Observe the iron filing patterns.

RESULTS The iron filings form a pattern of lines around the magnets. The long magnet has a buildup of filings around both ends.

WHY? A magnetic field is the area around a magnet in which the force of the magnet affects the movement of metal objects. The iron filings are pulled toward the magnets when they enter the magnetic field. The magnetic force increases as the filings near the magnet. The force field has equal strength around the round magnet, but the force fields at the ends of rectangular magnets are always stronger than the force fields in the middle of the magnets.

Force Field

ELECTROMAGNET

PURPOSE To demonstrate that an electric current produces a magnetic field.

MATERIALS wire, 18-gauge, insulated, 1 yard (1 m)
long iron nail
paper clips
6-volt battery
adult helper

PROCEDURE

1. Wrap the wire tightly around the nail, leaving about 6 inches (15 cm) of free wire on each end.

2. Have an adult strip the insulation off both ends of the wire.

3. Secure one end of the wire to one pole of the battery.

4. Touch the free end of the wire to the other battery pole while touching the nail to a pile of paper clips.

5. Lift the nail while keeping the ends of the wire on the battery pole.

6. When the nail starts to feel warm, disconnect the wire end you are holding against the battery pole.

RESULTS The paper clips stick to the iron nail.

WHY? There is a magnetic field around all wires carrying an electric current. Straight wires have a weak magnetic field around them. The strength of the magnetic field around the wire was increased by coiling the wire into a smaller space, placing a magnetic material—the nail—inside the coil of wire, and increasing the electrical flow through the wire—attaching a battery. The iron nail became magnetized and attracted the paper clips.

KEEPER

PURPOSE To determine how metals affect a magnetic field.

MATERIALS 4 small paper clips
aluminum foil
bar magnet
steel spatula

PROCEDURE

1. Lay the paper clips on a table and cover them with a sheet of aluminum foil.

2. Set the magnet on the foil over the clips.

3. Raise the magnet and observe any movement of the clips.

4. Position the clips so that they lay under the spatula.

5. Set the magnet on top of the spatula.

6. Lift the spatula with the magnet and observe any movement of the clips.

RESULTS The magnet attracts the paper clips through the aluminum foil. The magnet does not attract the paper clips through the steel spatula.

WHY? The magnetic force field passes through the aluminum, but the steel spatula restricts the movement of the force field. The steel spatula is attracted to the magnet, but the metal provides another path for the magnetic field. This new path is through and around the steel spatula. The steel keeps the lines of force closer to the magnetic field, acting as a barrier to other magnetic materials.

TILT

PURPOSE To demonstrate that objects in water have a different weight than they do in air.

MATERIALS

heavy string
scissors
ruler
2 washers
pencil

table
masking tape
marking pen
3 drinking glasses,
  8 ounces (250 ml)

PROCEDURE

1. Measure and cut two strings 12 inches (30 cm) long.

2. Tie one string around each end of the pencil.

3. Tie one washer to the end of each string.

4. Cut a string about 24 inches (60 cm) long.

5. Tie one end of the string around the center of the pencil and tape the free end to the edge of a table.

6. Move the position of the supporting string on the pencil until the pencil hangs parallel with the edge of the table. The washers should be about 4 inches (10 cm) above the floor.

7. Use tape and a marking pen to label two glasses as A and B.

8. Set the empty glasses on the floor so that one washer hangs inside each glass.

9. Fill a third glass with water from the faucet and slowly pour the water into glass A.

RESULTS When the water level touches the washer, the washer rises, the pencil tilts, and the washer in the empty glass is lowered.

WHY? Gravity pulls everything toward the center of Earth. This downward pull on the washers is referred to as their weight. The glasses appear to be empty but are actually filled with air. In air, the weight of the two washers is the same. Placing one of the balanced washers in water decreases its downward pull (weight) and causes the pencil to tilt toward the heavier side. The upward force exerted by water is called buoyancy.

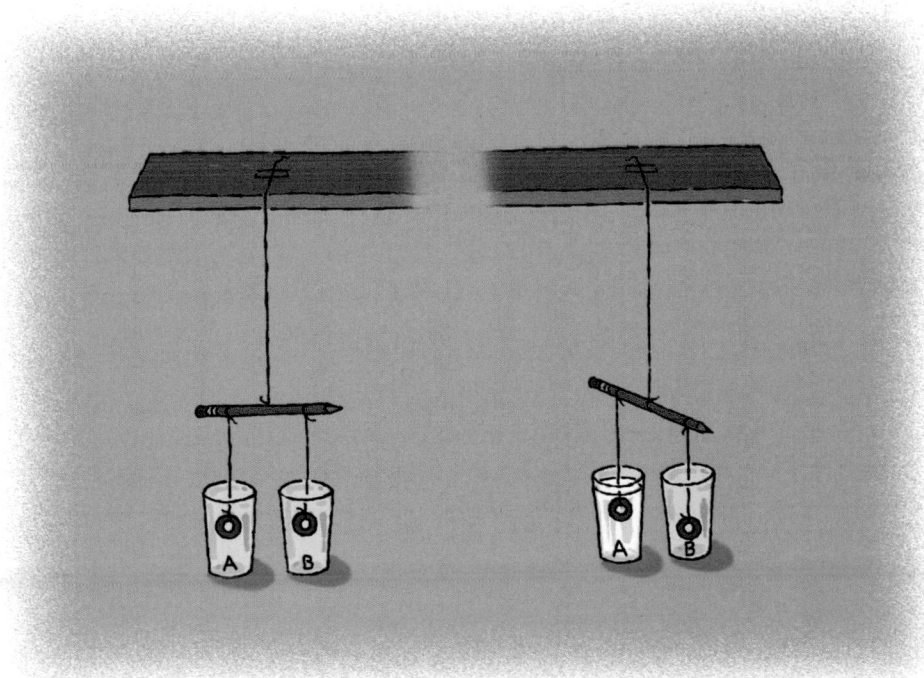

RISERS

PURPOSE To determine how the buoyancy of a substance can be changed.

MATERIALS drinking glass
club soda
modeling clay

PROCEDURE

1. Fill the drinking glass three-quarters full with soda.

2. Immediately add 5 tiny balls of clay one at a time.

3. The clay pieces must be about the size of a rice grain.

4. Wait and watch.

RESULTS Bubbles collect on the clay. The clay pieces rise to the surface, spin over, and fall to the bottom of the glass, where more bubbles start to stick to them again.

WHY? The soda contains carbon dioxide, which forms bubbles that stick to the clay. The clay balls initially sink because their weight is greater than the upward buoyant force. The gas bubbles act like tiny balloons that make the balls light enough to float to the surface. The carbon dioxide bubbles are knocked off at the surface, and the balls again sink to the bottom until more bubbles stick to them.

CLAY

CLUB
SODA

SHAPELY

PURPOSE To determine if shape affects the strength of an object.

MATERIALS 3 sheets of printer paper
transparent tape
light books, about 1 pound (454 g)

PROCEDURE

1. Fold the paper sheets into three shapes by following these steps:

» Shape A—fold one sheet in thirds and tape the edges together.
» Shape B—fold one sheet into fourths and tape the edges together.
» Shape C—roll one sheet into a cylinder and tape the edges together.

2. Stand each paper shape on a flat table.

3. Place one book at a time on top of each shape until it collapses.

4. Record the number of books that each paper shape can support.

RESULTS The rolled paper holds more books.

WHY? Gravity (a pull toward the center of Earth) pulls each book downward, and the paper structures push upward. If the upward push is less than the downward pull of gravity, the book crushes the paper structure. The open paper cylinder is the strongest of the shapes tested because the weight (force of gravity) of the supported book(s) is evenly distributed through the paper pillar.

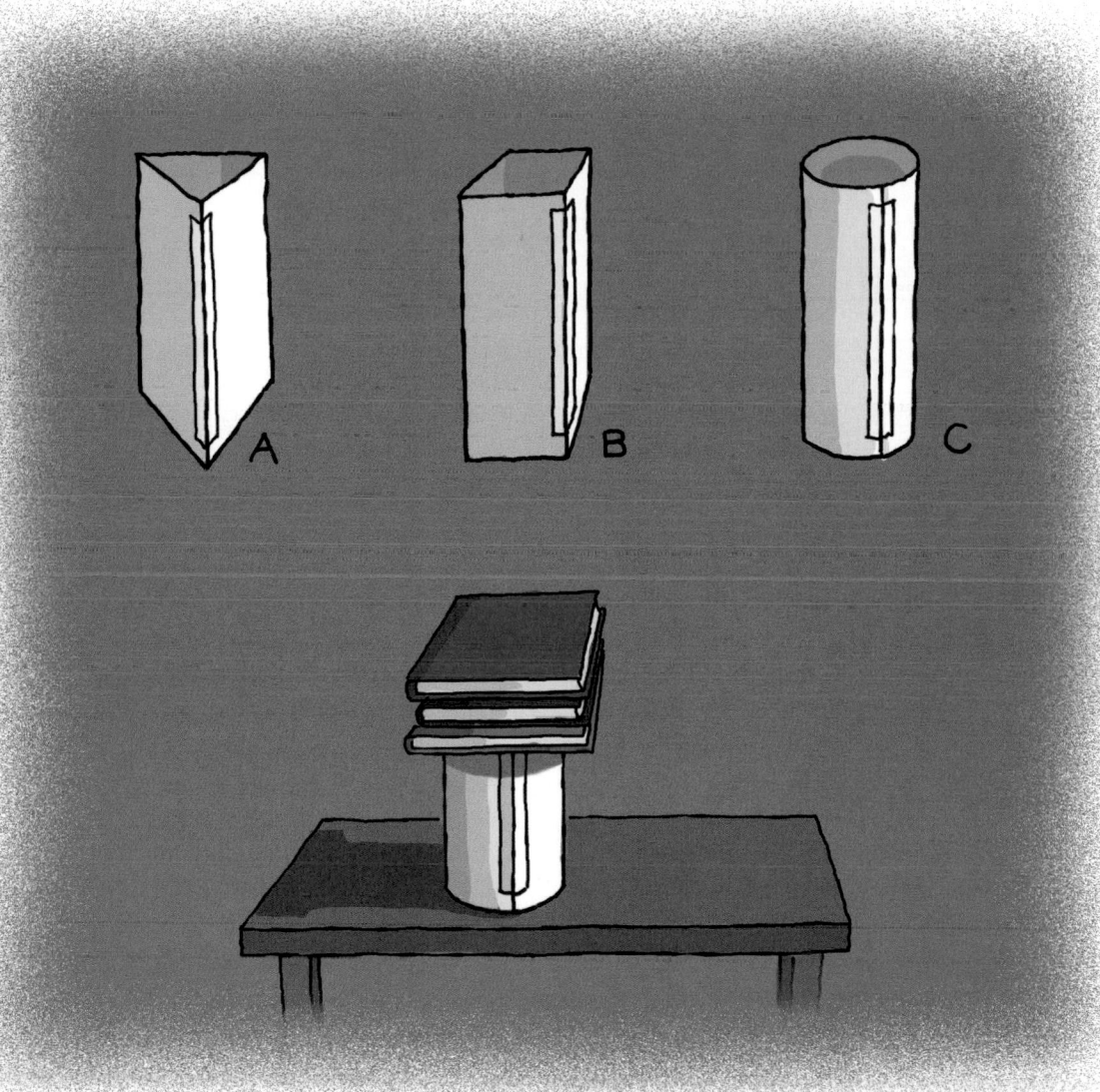

A

B

C

Up Hill

PURPOSE To determine the effect that an object's center of gravity has on motion.

MATERIALS 2 yardsticks (meter sticks)
3 books, each at least 1 inch (2.5 cm) thick
masking tape
2 funnels of equal size

PROCEDURE

1. Put two books 30 inches (75 cm) apart on the floor.

2. Place the remaining book on top of one of the other books.

3. Position the yardsticks on top of the books to form a V shape with the open part of the letter on the double book stack.

4. Tape the bowls of the funnels together.

5. Place the joined funnels at the bottom of the track formed by the yardsticks.

RESULTS The funnels roll up the hill.

WHY? The funnels are not defying the laws of gravity. Actually, as the joined funnels move, their center of gravity (the point where the weight is equally distributed) moves downward. Notice that the center of the joined funnels gets closer to the floor as it moves along the raised yardsticks.

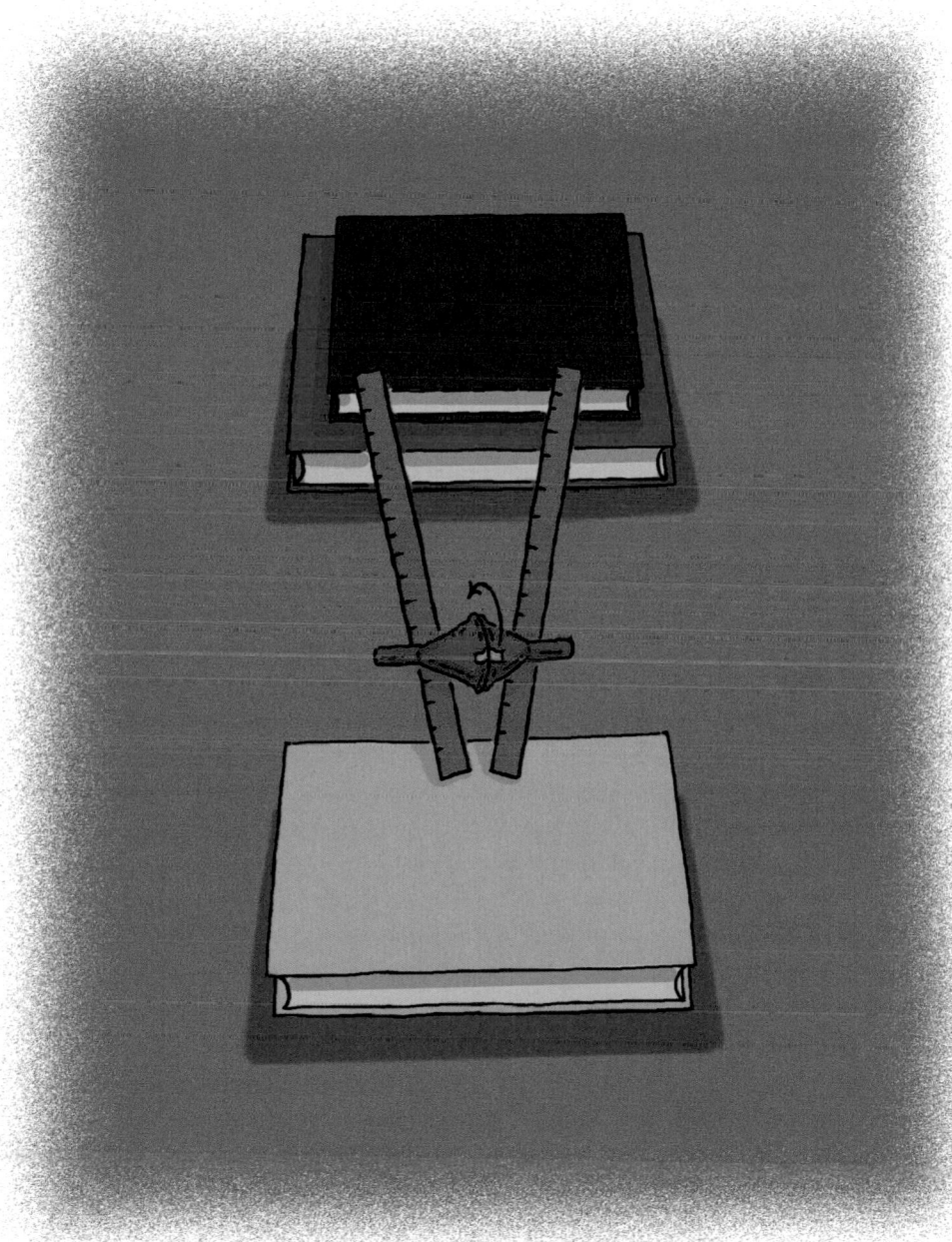

TIMER

PURPOSE To determine how the length of a pendulum affects the time of each swing.

MATERIALS

string
washer
scissors
ruler
table

heavy book
stopwatch
tape
helper

PROCEDURE

1. Measure and cut a string the height of the table.

2. Tie one end of the string to the washer, and use tape to attach the other end of the string to the end of the ruler.

3. Lay the ruler on the table with about 4 inches (10 cm) of the ruler extending over the edge, and the string hanging freely.

4. Lay the book on top of the ruler to hold it in place.

5. Pull the washer to one side and release it.

6. Ask your helper to start the timer as you count the number of swings in 10 seconds.

7. Shorten the string so that it is one-fourth its length.

8. Pull the washer to one side, release it, and count the number of swings in 10 seconds as your helper records the time.

RESULTS The number of swings doubles with the shorter string.

WHY? Galileo has been credited for discovering the relationship between the length of a pendulum and the time of its swing. The story told is that he observed the swinging of a great lamp while in church and timed the swings by comparing it with his pulse beat. He later discovered that the time of a swing depends on the length of the pendulum and that the time decreases by one-half if the string is one-fourth the original length.

OVER THE EDGE

PURPOSE To demonstrate that the center of gravity is the balancing point of an object.

MATERIALS string, 12 inches (30 cm)
yardstick (meter stick)
hammer (wooden-handled hammer works best)

PROCEDURE

1. Hold the ends of the sting together and tie a knot about 2 inches (5 cm) from the ends.

2. Insert the hammer and yardstick through the loop.

3. Position the end of the yardstick on a table's edge.

4. The handle of the hammer must touch the yardstick and the head of the hammer will extend under the table.

5. Change the position of the hammer until the whole unit—yardstick, string, and hammer—balances.

RESULTS The unit balances with only a small amount of the yardstick touching the table.

WHY? The hammer, string, and yardstick all act as a single unit with a center of gravity. The center of gravity is the point where any object balances. The dashed line in the diagram allows you to visualize the center of gravity. The heavy hammer head counterbalances the weight on the left side of the balancing point.

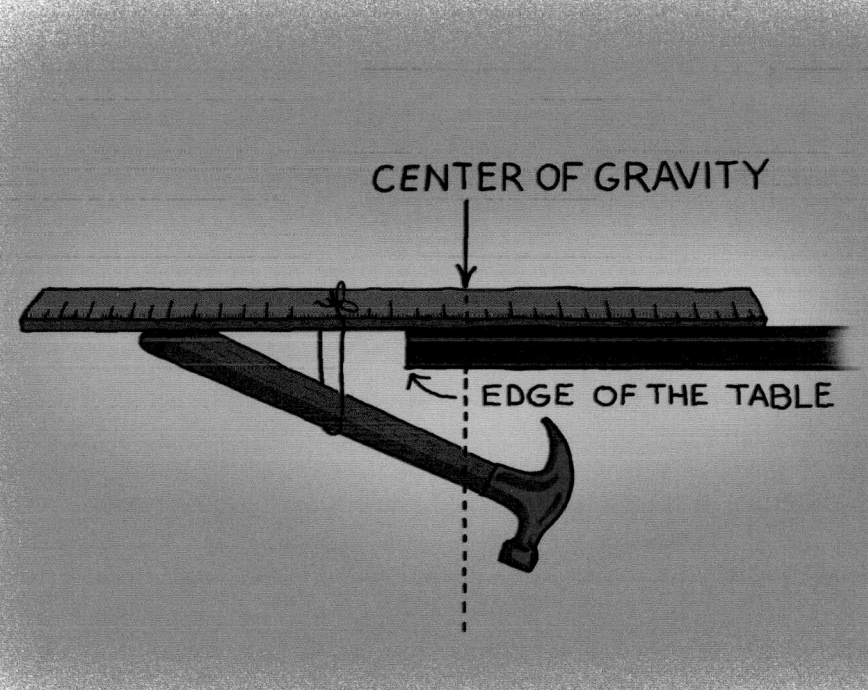

CENTER OF GRAVITY

EDGE OF THE TABLE

BALANCING ACT

PURPOSE To determine the center of gravity point.

MATERIALS modeling clay
2 metal forks
1 flat toothpick
drinking glass or wide-mouthed jar

PROCEDURE

1. Make a ball of clay about the size of a large marble.

2. Insert the tip of one of the forks into the clay ball.

3. Insert the second fork at about a 45-degree angle from the first fork.

4. Insert the pointed end of the toothpick in the clay between the forks.

5. Place the end of the toothpick on the edge of the glass. Move it further over the glass until the forks balance.

Note: Decrease the angle between the forks if they will not balance.

RESULTS There is one point at which the toothpick supports the weight of both forks and the clay.

WHY? The angle of the forks spreads their weight so that there is one place on the toothpick where all of the weight seems to be located. This spot is called the center of gravity.

Balancing Act

LIFT OFF

PURPOSE To demonstrate the effect of a kite's tail.

MATERIALS 1 sheet of notebook paper
scissors
transparent tape
string
ruler

PROCEDURE

1. Measure and cut a 2-inch x 12-inch (5-cm x 30-cm) strip from the sheet of paper.

2. Use tape to attach an 18-inch (45-cm) length of string to one end of the strip.

3. Hold the free end of the string and whip the paper back and forth in front of you.

4. Cut a ¼-inch x 12-inch (0.5-cm x 30-cm) strip from the paper and attach it with tape to the free end of the wider strip.

5. Again move the strip back and forth in front of you.

RESULTS The paper twirls around, but when the small strip is attached, the movement is smoother.

WHY? The paper moves forward at an angle, causing the air to flow faster over the top side. Fast-moving air has a lower pressure around the moving stream. Thus, more uplift is exerted on the bottom of the strip.

The angle of the paper is not constant, causing changes in the pressure along with a turbulent air flow across the strip. These changes make the strip twist and rotate. The paper tail makes the angle more constant. Therefore, there is a smoother flow of air across the paper and less twisting.

SHORTER

PURPOSE To determine how the length of a string affects the sound of a stringed instrument.

MATERIALS model stringed instrument from previous experiment
ruler

PROCEDURE

1. The buckets of your stringed instrument should be filled with rocks and the pencils should be near the edge of the table. Pluck the string and make a mental note of the sound heard.

2. Move the pencils about 12 inches (30 cm) apart and pluck the string again. Compare that sound with the sound previously heard.

3. Repeat step 2, moving the pencils about 6 inches (15 cm) apart.

RESULTS The plucked string produces a higher sound when the pencils are closer together.

WHY? Moving the pencils closer together has the same effect as shortening the string. The shorter the string, the faster it vibrates when plucked, and the higher the pitch of the sound produced. The same results occur when a string is shortened on a stringed instrument such as a guitar by holding down a string with one hand while plucking the string with the other.

Shorter

GLOSSARY

BUOYANCY The upward force exerted by a liquid such as water on any object in or on the liquid.

CENTER OF GRAVITY Point at which an object balances.

DIFFRACTION GRATING A material that disperses light.

DISPERSE To separate light into its spectrum colors by refraction.

EFFORT FORCE The push or pull needed to move an object.

ELECTRON The negatively charged particle in an atom.

GRAVITY A force that pulls toward the center of a celestial body, such as Earth.

INCLINED PLANE A slanting or sloping surface used to raise an object to a higher level.

MAGNETIC FIELD Area around a magnet in which the force of the magnet affects the movement of other magnetic objects; made up of invisible lines of magnetic force.

MOLECULE The smallest particle of a substance; made of one or more atoms.

NUCLEUS The central part of an atom.

PITCH The property of sound that makes it high or low; also, the distance between the ridges winding around a screw.

REFRACT To bend.

SIMPLE MACHINE A lever, inclined plane, wheel and axle, screw, wedge, or pulley.

SOUND A form of wave motion produced when objects vibrate.

STATIC ELECTRICITY A buildup of static charges in one place.

TENSION The condition of being stretched.

VIBRATE To move quickly back and forth.

VISIBLE SPECTRUM The colors found in white light: red, orange, yellow, green, blue, indigo, and violet.

WEIGHT The downward pull that gravity has on an object.

FOR MORE INFORMATION

Canadian Association of Physicists
  555 King Edward Avenue
  3rd Floor
  Ottawa, ON K1N 7N5
  Canada
  (613) 562-5614
  website: http://www.cap.ca
  Find out about careers in physics, enter the Art of Physics photography contest, or learn about student scholarships and prizes.

Intel
  2200 Mission College Boulevard
  Santa Clara, CA 95054-1549
  (408) 765-8080
  website: http://www.intel.com
  Read student profiles of winning research projects from the Intel International Science and Engineering Fair, and find educational material about Women in Science, tips for your science fair project, and links to other competitions.

National Science Foundation (NSF)
  4201 Wilson Boulevard
  Arlington, VA 22230
  (703) 292-5111
  website: http://www.nsf.gov
  The NSF is dedicated to science, engineering, and education. Learn how to be a Citizen Scientist, read about the latest scientific discoveries, and find out about the newest innovations in technology.

The Society for Science and the Public
Student Science
1719 N Street NW
Washington, DC 20036
(800) 552-4412
website: http://student.societyforscience.org
The Society for Science and the Public presents many science resources, such as science news for students, the latest updates on the Intel Science Talent Search and the Intel International Science and Engineering Fair, and information about cool jobs and doing science.

USA Science & Engineering Festival
Walter E. Washington Convention Center
801 Mt. Vernon Place NW
Washington, DC 20001
(202) 459-0880
website: http://www.usasciencefestival.org
The USA Science & Engineering Festival is a national grassroots effort to advance STEM education and inspire the next generation of scientists and engineers. Nationwide school programs, contests, and events year-round culminate in a two-day Grand Finale Expo, free of charge.

WEB SITES

Due to the changing nature of internet links, Rosen Publishing has developed an online list of Web sites related to the subject of this book. This site is updated regularly. Please use this link to access this list:

http://www.rosenlinks.com/JVCW/physic

FOR FURTHER READING

Ardley, Neil. *101 Great Science Experiments.* New York, NY: DK Ltd., 2014.

Buczynski, Sandy. *Designing a Winning Science Fair Project* (Information Explorer Junior). Ann Arbor, MI: Cherry Lake Publishing, 2014.

Datnow, Claire. *Edwin Hubble: Genius Discoverer of Galaxies* (Genius Scientists and their Genius Ideas). Berkeley Heights, NJ: Enslow Publishers, Inc., 2015.

Gardner, Robert. *A Kid's Book of Experiments with Stars* (Surprising Science Experiments). New York, NY: Enslow Publishing, 2016.

Gifford, Clive. *Astronomy, Astronauts, and Space Exploration* (Watch this Space!). New York, NY: Crabtree Publishing, 2016.

Greve, Tom. *Astronomers* (Scientists in the Field). North Mankato, MN: Rorke Educational Media, 2016.

Henneberg, Susan. *Creating Science Fair Projects with Cool New Digital Tools* (Way Beyond PowerPoint: Making 21st Century Presentations). New York, NY: Rosen Central, 2014.

Kawa, Katie. *Freaky Space Stories* (Freaky True Science). New York, NY: Gareth Stevens Publishing, 2016.

Kuskowski, Alex. *Stargazing* (Out of this World). Minneapolis, MN: Super Sandcastle, 2016.

Levy, Joel. The *Universe Explained* (Guide for Curious Minds). New York, NY: Rosen Publishing, 2014.

McGill, Jordan. *Space Science Fair Projects* (Science Fair Projects). New York, NY: AV2 by Weigl, 2012.

Riggs, Kate. *Moons* (Across the Universe). Mankato, MN: Creative Education/Creative Paperbacks, 2015.

Rockett, Paul. *70 Thousand Million, Million, Million Stars in Space* (The Big Countdown). Chicago, IL: Capstone Raintree, 2016.

Saucier, C. A. P. *Explore the Cosmos Like Neil DeGrasse Tyson: A Space Science Journey.* Amherst, NY: Prometheus Books, 2015.

Spilsbury, Louise. *Space* (Make and Learn). New York, NY: PowerKids Press, 2015.

INDEX

A
air flow, 52-53
airplane, 30-31
atom, 26-27, 30-31

B
buoyancy, 39, 40

E
Earth, 39, 42
electric current, 34
electromagnetic, 34-35
electrons, 26, 28

F
flight, 30-31
fulcrum, 8

G
Galileo, 47
gravity
    center of, 42, 44, 48, 50
    effect (pull) of, 31, 39, 42
    laws of, 44
    weight, 39, 42

H
hair, 26-27

I
inclined plane, 12-13

K
kite, 52-53

L
lever, 8
light
    color spectrum, 14-15
    diffracting grating, 16-17
    dispersal, 15
    refraction, 15
    strobe effect, 18-19

M
magnets, 30-31, 32
magnetic force, 30, 36-37
magnetic field, 32, 34-35, 36-37
molecules, 22-23

N
nucleus, 26

P
pendulum, 46-47
pressure (air movement), 52-53
pump, 10-11